To Harry — wishing him lots of ice creams
and lots of stories to lick them to
    —M.M.

To Mum and Dad
    —J.A.

Text copyright © 1999 by Margaret Mahy
Illustrations copyright © 1999 by Jonathan Allen

First American edition 1999 published by Orchard Books
Published simultaneously in Great Britain by Frances Lincoln Limited

Margaret Mahy and Jonathan Allen assert the moral right
to be identified as the author and illustrator of this work.

Orchard Books, A Grolier Company
95 Madison Avenue, New York, NY 10016

Manufactured in China by Imago Publishing Ltd.
A Vanessa Hamilton Book
Book design by Mark Foster

The text of this book is set in Centaur.
The illustrations are line and gouache on board.

10 9 8 7 6 5 4 3 2 1

Library of Congress Cataloging-in-Publication Data
Mahy, Margaret.
Simply delicious! / by Margaret Mahy; illustrated by Jonathan
Allen.—1st American ed.
p. cm.
Summary: A resourceful father engages in all kinds of acrobatic moves to keep
an assortment of jungle creatures from getting the double-dip-chocolate-chip-and-cherry
ice cream cone he is taking home to his son.
ISBN 0-531-30181-8 (alk. paper)
[1. Ice cream cones—Fiction. 2. Jungle animals—Fiction.]
I. Allen, Jonathan, ill. II. Title.
PZ7.M2773Si 1999
[E]—dc21 98-46185

Simply Delicious!

Margaret Mahy

drawings by Jonathan Allen

Orchard Books

New York

One evening, as he rode home on his faithful bike, Mr. Minky stopped at Muffin's Corner Shop and bought a double-dip-chocolate-chip-and-cherry ice cream with rainbow twinkles and chopped-nut sprinkles for his little boy, Finnegan. "Now, how will I get this double-dip-chocolate-chip-and-cherry ice cream home before it melts?" he wondered. "I know! I'll take a short cut down the lumpy, bumpy, jungle track. It runs right into my own back garden."

Mr. Minky bounded onto his bike and shot off along the jungle track. Giant bamboos arched over his head. Leaves as large as dinner plates brushed against his busy, bicycling knees. Mr. Minky lifted the ice cream high into the air to keep it safe and waved it around to keep it cool.

Two butterflies, sipping honey from a rare orchid, saw the ice cream lumping and bumping along below them.

"I like the look of that double-dip-chocolate-chip-and-cherry ice cream with rainbow twinkles and chopped-nut sprinkles," one butterfly said to the other. "Simply delicious!" the other replied.

Off they fluttered at bicycle speed, hovering over the ice cream and trying to land on it. Mr. Minky began swinging the double-dip-chocolate-chip-and-cherry ice cream in circles, hoping to baffle the butterflies while keeping the ice cream cool. A toucan, perched on a swaying bamboo, saw the ice cream bumping along the track below.

"I love the look of that double-dip-chocolate-chip-and-cherry ice cream with rainbow twinkles and chopped-nut sprinkles," tweedled the toucan. "Simply delicious!" And it dived and darted at the ice cream.

Mr. Minky, biking hard, swept his left
hand down and held the double-dip-
chocolate-chip-and-cherry ice cream
at knee level, waving it in circles to
baffle the butterflies, taunt the toucan —
and keep the ice cream cool. The butterflies
fluttered, the toucan dived, and Mr. Minky
bounced up and down, up and down, as
he biked along the lumpy, bumpy,
jungle track.

A spider monkey, peering out from under the creepers, saw the ice cream lumping and bumping by only inches from its nose.

"I love the look of that double-dip-chocolate-chip-and-cherry ice cream with rainbow twinkles and chopped-nut sprinkles," said the spider monkey. "Simply delicious!" And down it swooped on the ice cream.

Mr. Minky whipped the ice cream
up once more, holding it straight
out in front of him. Then he
waved it up and down to
baffle the butterflies, taunt
the toucan, muddle the
monkey — and keep
the ice cream cool.

The butterflies fluttered,
the toucan dived, the monkey
swooped, and Mr. Minky bounced
up and down, up and down, as
he biked along the lumpy,
bumpy, jungle track.

A ferocious tiger,
glowering in its lair,
saw the ice cream
speeding by.

"I like the look of that double-dip-chocolate-
chip-and-cherry ice cream with rainbow
twinkles and chopped-nut sprinkles,"
snarled the tiger. "Simply delicious!"
And it sprang at the ice cream.

But Mr. Minky quickly tossed it from his left hand
to his right, catching it in midair. Holding it
at arm's length, he swung it from side to
side, hoping to baffle the butterflies,
taunt the toucan, muddle the monkey,
trick the tiger — and keep the ice cream
cool. The butterflies fluttered, the
toucan dived, the spider monkey
swooped, the tiger sprang, and
Mr. Minky bounced up and
down, up and down, as he
biked along the lumpy,
bumpy, jungle track.

A huge crocodile was sunning itself on the
river-bank. In between leaves as large as
dinner plates, it saw the ice cream
sweeping by.

"I love the look of that double-dip-chocolate-chip-and-cherry ice cream with rainbow twinkles and chopped-nut sprinkles," croaked the crocodile. "Simply delicious!" And it lunged at the ice cream.

But Mr. Minky tossed the ice cream
high into the air. As it came down,
he cleverly caught it
on his toe,

kicked it up into the air again,
caught it on his elbow,
flicked it high,
tilted his head back,
then caught it once more —
this time, on his nose!

The butterflies fluttered, the toucan dived, the spider monkey
swooped, the tiger sprang, the crocodile lunged, and
Mr. Minky kicked right and left, keeping them
at bay, bouncing up and down,
up and down, while balancing
the ice cream on his nose
as he biked along the
lumpy, bumpy,
jungle track.

At long last he burst
out of the jungle, shot up his
home-made ramp, and, flying
through the air across the back
fence, glided gracefully into
his own back garden.
Little Finnegan ran
to meet him.

Mr. Minky tossed his head, caught the ice cream as it flew through the air, and held it out to Finnegan.

Seeing the double-dip-chocolate-chip-and-cherry
ice cream with rainbow twinkles and chopped-nut
sprinkles, Finnegan shouted with happiness.
He swept his tongue across it in grand style.
"Simply delicious!" he yelled.

"I feel quite
hungry myself," said
Mr. Minky, smiling at
Finnegan's joy.

HUNGRY!

The crocodile looked at the tiger
and licked his lips.
The tiger looked at the spider monkey
and licked his lips.
The spider monkey looked at the toucan
and licked his lips.
The toucan looked at the butterflies
and clicked his beak.

"Simply delicious!" they cried,
and began chasing one another
back through the jungle along
the lumpy, bumpy track.

Mr. Minky put his bike in the shed
and went in to dinner – spicy pie
and scrumptious pudding . . .